DATE DUE			

$12.95   5485

E
Le

Leigh, Oretta

The merry-go-round

 GUMDROP BOOKS - Bethany, Missouri

The Merry-Go-Round

The Merry-Go-Round

Oretta Leigh

illustrated by
Kathryn E. Shoemaker

Holiday House / New York

Library of Congress Cataloging in Publication Data

Leigh, Oretta.
    The merry-go-round.

    Summary: As the merry-go-round goes round and round,
the animals all go up and down, the children ride, some
two by two—everyone enjoys the animal zoo.
    1. Children's stories, American. [1. Merry-go-round—
Fiction. 2. Stories in rhyme]   I. Shoemaker, Kathryn E.,
ill.   II. Title.
PZ8.3.L534Me   1985   [E]   84-15731
ISBN 0-8234-0544-3

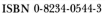

To *Lenore, Eileen* and *Lila*

The merry-go-round
goes round and round.

The animals all go
up and down
and up and down.

The children all ride
one by one

and two by two

and three by three

and side by side.

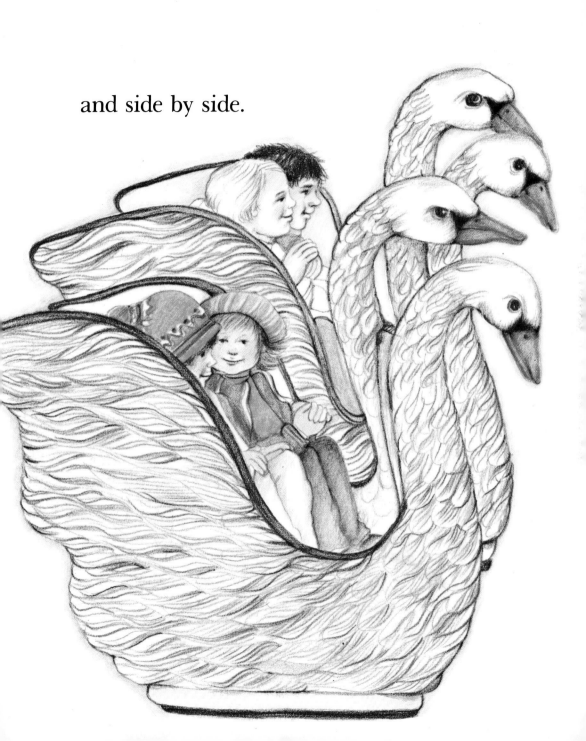

Mothers and fathers
and grandpas, too,

and uncles and aunts
and Cousin Sue

and sisters and brothers

and Baby Lou
all like to ride
on the animal zoo.

The lions roar.

The horses neigh.

The tigers growl.

The giraffes sigh.

The panthers snarl.

The roosters crow.

The dogs bark.

The cats meow.

Round and round
and round and round,

up and down
goes the merry-go-round.

The music stops,
the animals too.

Then everyone leaves
the animal zoo.